DINO
WARS
Rise of the Raptors

For Floyd and Cora Whitehouse - DM
For Olive, my dinosaur loving daughter - AB

Dino Wars: Book 1, Rise of the Raptors
An original concept by author Dan Metcalf
© Dan Metcalf, 2018

The right of Dan Metcalf to be identified as the author of this work has been
asserted by him in accordance with the Copyright, Designs and Patents Act 1988

Illustrations by Aaron Blecha
© Aaron Blecha, 2018
Represented by The Bright Agency
www.thebrightagency.com

Published by MAVERICK ARTS PUBLISHING LTD
Studio 3a, City Business Centre, 6 Brighton Road,
Horsham, West Sussex, RH13 5BB
+44 (0) 1403 256941
© Maverick Arts Publishing Limited April 2018

A CIP catalogue record for this book is available
at the British Library.

ISBN: 978-1-84886-319-4

DINO
WARS
Rise of the Raptors

DAN METCALF
illustrated by **Aaron Blecha**

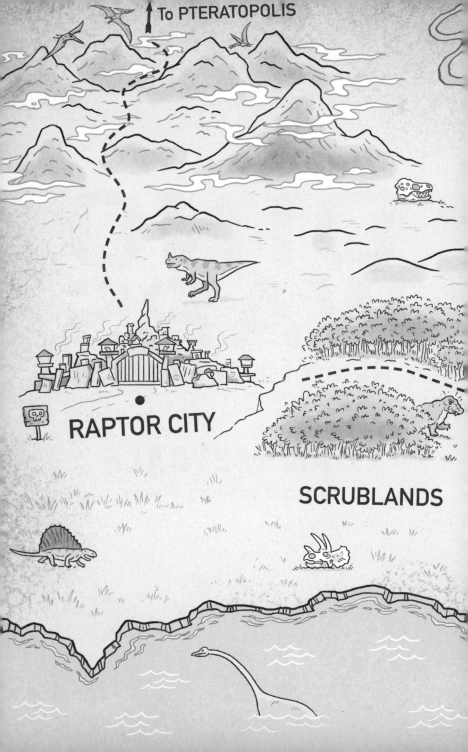

Chapter One.

"Okay everyone. You understand the mission objective?" said Adam. His friends were gathered around him in a huddle, speaking in low, secretive tones. His sister Chloe gave a bored eye-roll and a nod. Twins Benji and Tuppence, just six years old and full of energy, gave an enthusiastic thumbs up. Dag gave a nod; as an iguanodon, he had no thumbs, just bony claws that he used for eating and cutting things.

"Can I suggest something?" he whispered, holding up a rickety-looking, home-made gadget. "I've managed to fashion this grabber claw from some old bits of machinery. It has a very long reach, so we could hide in the bushes and extend it out to its full length. It can get anything in its pincers!"

Benji and Tuppence laughed.

"Ha! You'd have no chance! Leave it to us," said Tuppence.

"We can tunnel underneath the location and snatch the target from below. It should take us four or five hours maximum," said Benji, his arms crossed. Tuppence mirrored him.

"The only problem is that you are not, in fact, moles," said Chloe, "however muddy you like to get. I don't see why we can't just go and see Ella and ask for our ball back?"

Adam looked over to his football, trapped in the centre of a carefully maintained

field of cabbages and then back over to his sister. It hadn't actually occurred to him to do that. That was one reason he loved and detested Chloe at the same time. She was a know-it-all. Adam often thought that when she was born, she had received most of their mother's qualities. She had the same light brown hair, pale skin and freckles. She had the same dimple in her cheek when she smiled and she was almost always right. It was one of her most annoying features.

"Because... because... it's boring!" he protested. "Anyway, she's a five metre tall diplodocus and very precious about her crops. We're likely to get stomped!"

"But I invented this grabber especially," said Dag. "I don't see why we can't–"

"I'm telling you, underground is the best way..." interrupted Benji.

And the crowd of kids fell into an argument

once again. Adam sighed as they all bickered and quarrelled.

"If you want something doing, you have to do it yourself," he muttered to himself. It was something his dad had always said and now Adam knew what it meant. He left the group and set off at a sprint.

"Adam, no!" called Chloe, but it was too late. He was already a blur of blond hair, stomping across the field and knocking over cabbages. He grinned as he ran.

"Oi!" came a call from across the field. Suddenly the sun was blocked out by a huge dinosaur rising up from the ground. Ella, a large brown diplodocus, had been asleep under a shelter until she had heard the clomping of boots on her soil.

Her long, long, neck stretched out until she could see Adam, who had stopped in fear, just metres from the ball. "Get off my land!" she bellowed.

Adam dived for the ball and scooped it up, tucking it under his arm.

"RUN!" he yelled, but his friends had already begun to move.

He ran off the field and down a green spit of grass between the allotment plots.

THUD! THUD! THUD! came the sound of Ella behind him. She was slow, but her size meant that she could run a few hundred metres with just a few steps.

"Adam! To me!" said Tuppence, running alongside him. He threw the ball to her and she peeled off to the side. Adam kept running.

"Blinking kids!" called Ella. "Keep off my allotment!" She continued to chase Adam, uninterested in the ball itself. Breathless, he found an extra pocket of energy from somewhere and dashed forwards. "Come 'ere!"

Adam sped through Bastion, the village of mud huts, wood cabins and farmsteads that his parents had helped to build. Around him, the humans and dinosaurs who lived and worked together turned to look at him as he sped past them, pursued by a giant, angry diplodocus. Of course, this was nothing new to them; just that pesky Adam Caine getting into trouble again...

But soon he had reached the limits of the settlement, marked by a natural stone wall; part of a cliff that his father had built around as a natural defence from the world outside. There was nowhere to go, except...

Looking about, he spied a small opening in the cliff ahead. Not a cave exactly, but large enough to hide himself inside. He ran to it.

"Come out here, Caine!" said Ella.

"Um... no thanks!" Adam called. She was too

large to get anywhere near the small cave. Adam congratulated himself on hiding well, but then realised that he would have to come out sometime and Ella could wait all night.

"Hey!" came a call. Adam recognised Benji's voice. "Over here!"

Peeking out from his hidey-hole, Adam saw Ella turn her massive neck in time to get a football on the nose.

"Oof!" she called. "Ow!" she said again, this time lifting up one huge leg. Adam looked down to see a mechanical grabbing claw nip her on the back of the ankle. "You rotters!" She turned away from Adam and towards Chloe, Dag and the twins, who had come to distract her.

"Come and get us, bone-brain!" called Tuppence.

Ella turned her whole body and her massive tail thrashed about, narrowly missing the twins, but bashing straight into the cliff face of the gorge. The rocks rumbled and Adam heard a loud sound from behind him. The cave was shifting! The stones in the small passageway tumbled.

"I've had enough of you little beggars!" called Ella. She stomped off back towards the centre of Bastion.

"Woo-hoo!" yelled the twins. "Victory!" They danced around and high-fived Dag and Chloe. Adam, meanwhile, could see something in the corner of the cave. He fished a wind-up flashlight out of his pocket, a piece of oldtech that he had found when ploughing a field. It still worked and a few turns of the little handle later, he had light.

"Guys!" he shouted to his friends. "You *have* to come and see this!"

Chapter Two.

"It's a...it's a...what *is* it?" asked Benji.

"It's a door," said Dag. "It's a door where there should be no door."

And it was. The large steel slab was riveted around the edge and had a wheel at the centre that Adam supposed you had to turn to enter. The strange thing was – where could it lead to? The cave itself was in a natural cliff; the only thing behind it should be solid rock. *Only one way to find out*, thought Adam.

He placed his hand on the wheel – but it was instantly slapped away by Chloe.

"What do you think you're doing?" she

snapped.

"Just taking a look. Aren't you curious to see what's inside?" he said. He couldn't stop the mischievous grin from spreading across his face. Chloe floundered.

"No! Alright, maybe a bit... but it could be dangerous!"

"If it was dangerous, there would be a 'danger' sign on the door," reasoned Benji.

"We should get Tora," said Chloe. "She's the leader, she should be the one to open it."

Adam considered it, but the call to adventure was too strong.

"Chloe, we've lived in Bastion our entire lives. Don't you think we have a right to know where a hidden door in *our* village goes to?"

Chloe looked to Dag for some back-up.

"Sorry Chloe," he shrugged, "I *really* want to know."

"Fine!" Chloe shouted, throwing up her

hands. "But if you get caved in, don't come running to me!"

Adam and Dag smiled. The two friends put their hands on the wheel and turned it. It was stiff, but Dag was stronger than he looked. His dinosaur arms were built for pulling down small trees and he often used them to bend metal salvaged from oldtech into grand contraptions. Tuppence and Benji made themselves useful by clearing loose rock from the floor and soon they were able to open the door outwards enough to squeeze though.

"Right then," said Adam, taking a deep breath. "Into the unknown!"

With his trusty wind-up flashlight at arm's length in front of him, Adam stepped forward. The tunnel ahead was narrow, but tall enough for them all to stand up straight.

"This has been carved out of the rock," said Dag. He ran a claw down the wall, leaving a mark. "Sandstone. Easy to tunnel through."

They came to a turn in the tunnel and Adam found a bank of light switches on the wall. He carefully flicked them on, one by one. Each flick of a switch lit up a new red light from bulbs hanging down from the ceiling. Adam found himself on a metal balcony, overlooking a large cavern which had been carved into the rock. Desks and chairs filled the space and a table in the centre held a large map, littered with toy soldiers like a child's playroom.

"It's massive!" shouted Tuppence, her voice echoing through the cavern. She and Benji ran down a metal staircase, clanging on every step

"Shhh!" said Chloe.

"There's no one here, Chloe," said Dag, following the twins down the steps and walking amongst the desks. He peered over the paperwork that lay abandoned. "No one has been here for years."

Chloe looked down on the immense space. Although it was clear that Dag was right, she still couldn't bring herself to speak in anything more than a whisper.

"It looks like a war room," she said. "Just like the ones the humans built to protect themselves during the Dino Wars."

"How do you know that?" asked Adam. He too jumped down the steps to take a look. Chloe, the only one left on the balcony, hesitantly walked down.

"The library in Bastion has more than just old adventure books you know," laughed Dag. "It's in the *Complete History of the Dino Wars*."

Adam smiled and shook his head in disbelief. He sometimes couldn't believe that he and Dag were best friends, as they were so different. If they hadn't been raised by the same foster family in Bastion after their parents died, they may never have met at all, but Adam was glad that

they had.

He walked up a few steps to a platform where the desks were lined with machinery and screens. He trailed a finger across the screens, leaving a line in the years of dust.

"Don't touch anything!" warned Chloe. Adam raised an eyebrow and defiantly drummed his fingers on the panel. "We don't know what all this stuff *does*!"

"It's useless oldtech, that's all," said Adam. He walked up to a plate in the centre of the desk shaped like a hand print and placed his own hand on it absently. "It'll have been dead for years."

"Actually, Adam, that looks like–" but Dag was cut short:

"Ow!" said Adam. "It pricked me!"

Suddenly the red lights around the bunker changed to bright white, blinding them. The sound of humming increased as computers around them awakened, bleeping and whirring into life.

"It weren't us!" said Tuppence.

"We didn't touch nothin'!" said Benji, leaping up from under a desk.

"<Bzt!> H-hello – ooo. M-my name is <fzzzz> HUM3000," came a voice from around them. It was being piped in through speakers in the room and had a tinny, electric sound to it.

"Allied DNA D-detected. <gzt!> Welcome baaaack General Caine!"

Chloe stepped up to the platform with Dag and raised an eyebrow to Adam.

"I told you not to touch anything..."

"What? I'm not General Caine!" said Adam. He looked at his finger which was bleeding from a small pinprick. "I'm *Adam* Caine."

"It must be the computer for this place. It detects the DNA and identifies you. Is that right, computer?" Dag asked.

"Affirmative. Blood s-sample detected and identified as <bzt!> General Caesar Caine of the Allied Human Forces."

Chloe looked up.

"*Caesar* Caine? It means our dad. It's mistaken you for Dad, Adam!" she said. Adam smiled. He barely remembered their dad anymore. It was heartening to know that he could be mistaken for the man he thought of as a hero.

"It's got a glitch," said Dag, peering at the screen below him, listing lines and lines of code. "Probably from being buried underground. Even a father and son don't have the same DNA. Similar, but not the same."

"General Caine, you have <GZZZ!> one message saved," said the HUM3000 computer. The voice stuttered and slurred now and then, as though it was still trying to wake up from its long sleep. Adam shrugged.

"Okay. Play message," he said. "Looks like I'm playing Dad today!" A chirpy 'ping' sound confirmed that the message was about to be played. A huge screen high above them burst into life.

"Message now <bzt!> playing. Message received from MARCUS GREEN, twelve years, nine months and eight days ago."

"Marcus Green?" said Dag.

"Who?" asked Adam.

An image of a man in military uniform flashed up on the screen. He was pale and tired looking, his eyes red around the rims.

"Hello Caesar. If you are watching this it means that the unthinkable has happened."

Chloe and Adam instinctively moved to be closer to each other. They reached out for each other's hand. "Marcus Green was head of the humans in the Dino Wars," said Chloe. "He died before we were born."

"The Dinosaur Army have won the war," he continued. "They have been far stronger than we ever thought they would be. They are excellent warriors. They can also be vicious and ruthless."

"Hey! My best friend's a dino!" said Adam. Dag looked somewhat proud, but Chloe shushed him.

"Which is why," said the image of Marcus Green, "the leaders of the Humans have decided

to put in place a fail-safe. We call it the Coda Program."

"Uh-oh," whispered Chloe.

"The Coda Program is a biological weapon we have developed. We have programmed a robotic laboratory in the West to make enough microspores to kill all the dinosaurs on Earth. It will release the spores into the atmosphere and the global winds will spread them around the planet."

Adam and Chloe stood with their mouths wide open in shock.

"What? Why?" said Adam. The image on the screen appeared to answer his question.

"If the dinosaurs have reclaimed the planet, we think it will mean that they hunt down and destroy all human life. With the Coda Program, we choose to destroy all dinosaurs instead of leaving them to ravage the planet. We thought we could control the dinosaurs, but they are stronger than we thought."

Chloe walked over to the video wall, her face red.

"You stupid, stupid man!" she yelled. "Just because you couldn't find peace doesn't mean that we couldn't!"

"He can't hear you!" shouted Adam. Marcus Green continued.

"It falls to you, Caesar, as General of the Allied Human Forces, to give the order." A large screen to their right flickered on and showed a white laboratory, entirely staffed by robotic arms, poised over test tubes and petri dishes with syringes. Words in the corner of the screen flashed 'Live Feed'. Green continued: "Once the lab has begun to make the spores, it will take four weeks to produce enough to rid the planet of the dinosaur race. In the event that the Coda Program has been armed too soon, the instructions in the disarmament manual should be followed. I leave this responsibility to you, my friend. I do not think I have long left to live."

"I thought he looked ill..." muttered Dag.

"Good luck, humankind."

The image on the screen faded.

"So..." began Adam, trying to process all the information. "The dinosaurs were winning the Dino Wars and Dad was supposed to release a bug that would kill them all?"

"Instead, he closed off this bunker, buried the only door to it and built a village outside it," said Chloe.

"Where humans could try to live together with peace-loving herbivores," said Dag. "That's so cool! He must have finally realised that obliterating the dinos wouldn't have solved anything. Respect to your dad!"

Adam and Chloe shared a proud glance.

"Yeah, pretty cool."

The screens on the central console started to fizz and buzz. The lights dimmed.

"General Caine, we are experiencing power difficulties," said the computer. Its tinny voice wavered. "Do you give permission for me to take full control?"

Adam laughed.

"I'm still not General Caine, but yeah, go ahead!"

The computer was silent for a second.

"Security question: Name of first born son?"

"Easy!" he smiled. "Adam!"

"Thank you," said the computer. "Please confirm: you are relinquishing control to the HUM3000 system?"

"Yes!" said Adam, impatiently. "Get on with it!"

Dag looked over the screens.

"Oh," he said. "Oh, dear..."

"Control regained!" said the computer.

"Power stabilised. Coda Program initiated."

Everyone froze.

"What?" said Adam. "Coda Program? The big dino-death bug thing? WHY?"

The computer's blank screens popped and buzzed.

"You have <gzt!> given full control to the HUM3000 system, General Caine."

"Control to sort out the power, not create a bio-weapon!" Adam shouted. "Stop the Coda Program! NOW!" He dashed to the large screen that showed the live feed of the laboratory. The robotic arms were creaking into life, slowly swivelling and injecting spores into test tubes. In a panic, Adam's temper got a hold of him and he unleashed a huge kick into the central part of the console.

Big mistake.

Dag and Chloe fell back as a large bang came from the casing of the console, sparks flying out.

Adam covered his eyes.

"Force is n-not n-necessary..." said the HUM3000. More sparks came from the computer console and Adam backed away.

"Adam! Get out of there!" called Tuppence.

"Stop the Coda Program!" Adam called. "Now! I am your General!"

"Caaaaaan nooooooot compuuuute..." came the reply. The console burst into flames.

Dag dragged his friend away from the console.

"It's malfunctioned, Adam!" he yelled. "It's been buried underground for years. The consoles could all blow! We need to get out!"

Chloe started to run around the desks, tipping over papers.

"What are you doing?" called Adam.

"You heard the man. Somewhere here there is a manual that can stop it. Get looking!"

Adam and Dag worked through each desk

one by one. They were no closer to finding it when a rumble shook the desks. "Get out, now!" screamed Adam.

Chloe ran to the steps to get to the balcony. Adam followed, noticing huge cracks forming in the walls around him. He had to hurry. There was a risk that the walls would cave in and they would all be buried alive.

"Adam, come on!" yelled Chloe. He pushed

the twins up the steps but noticed a small desk tucked underneath them that they hadn't searched. He quickly looked over the contents and spied a manual with a front cover that read:

Coda Program: DISARMAMENT

He leapt forward and grabbed the book. He sped up the steps two at a time and followed Dag and Chloe, running out of the tunnel and back out into the light. A large BOOM shook the ground and a cloud of dust followed them out of the door.

They stared at the hole where the bunker had once been.

"Oops," said Tuppence.

Chapter Three.

Adam and Chloe trudged through the mud, Adam holding the manual in his hand.

"Do you think it was all true?" he said. A part of him was clinging onto the hope that the video had been just a huge prank. "Perhaps it was just a trick, in case dinosaurs invaded the war office? They'd show them the message and..." he trailed off. Chloe, streaked with mud from their escape, shook her head.

They walked through Bastion, followed by Dag and the twins. People and dinosaurs looked at them as they passed. News travelled fast in the settlement and word soon got around that the son and daughter of one of their founders had been up to no good. They passed their hut and Chloe turned to go in. Adam caught her arm.

"I thought we were going home, to clean up?" she said. It was Adam's turn to shake his head.

"There's no time. We need to speak to Tora."

Tora was the oldest dinosaur in Bastion and perhaps even the oldest on New Earth. She was a seismosaurus, who at forty metres long, was one of the largest dinosaurs to have ever lived. She was retired now and rarely came out of the huge cave where she slept. The community of Bastion brought her gifts and food to take care of her. She had been one of the first dinosaurs in Bastion and had been great friends with Adam and Chloe's parents.

They approached the cave and Chloe rang the gong that stood outside it.

"I hope she's in," said Adam with a weak

grin.

"She's sixteen metres tall. I think we would have noticed if she had popped out for a jog," said Chloe. An echoing yawn came from the cave.

"Who's there?" came the voice. "Is it dinnertime already?"

"Tora, it's me. Chloe Caine," said Chloe.

"And Adam," said Adam. "We need to speak to you."

A grey head emerged out of the dark of the cave, blinking into the light. It was followed by a huge neck which was as thick as a tree trunk.

"My dears! It's been so long!" Tora smiled. She peered at them with her failing eyesight. "My goodness, how you've grown! Adam, you are the spitting image of your father. As for you young lady, how beautiful you look! Erm... but a little bit muddy..."

Adam smiled. Tora was the closest thing he

had to a grandmother figure. If she had been human she would be pinching his cheek and forcing sweets on him by now.

"Tora, we found something," he said.

"Oh?" she said. Her head rose further and she stepped out of the cave. Her immense feet thudded on the ground as she walked. Chloe gulped. She loved Tora but her sheer size always amazed her.

"What do you know about the Coda Program?" asked Dag, getting to the point. Tora's smile faded and she let out a long sigh. "Is it real?"

She nodded.

"It was just a rumour for a long time, one which the Dino Army refused to believe. When we were fighting the Dino Wars no one thought that the Human Army could be so ridiculous."

"Turns out, we were," said Chloe. "We found the war rooms and saw a message from Marcus

Green."

Tora stepped a few more paces and sat down in the sun.

"Marcus Green was a genius and it ran in the family. It was his father, Lucius Green, who was asked to come up with a new weapon to use in wartime. He brought back the dinosaurs. We had been long extinct of course but he recreated us and gave us better brains so we could talk, think and fight."

"But you rebelled," said Chloe. Tora nodded.

"We were capable of speech, thought and emotions and soon wondered why we were being treated like slaves. We rebelled and fought against the humans, led by the carnivores of course, and so it became known as the Dino Wars. Humans fought ancient, giant reptiles. We slowly won battles and land and brought an end to the war. We renamed the planet 'New Earth' to show a new power was in charge. By this point the Dino Army far outnumbered the humans. Lucius Green had long since died and his son Marcus felt guilty about his father creating us and became obsessed with finding a way to stop us. Your father served in the army under him."

"But I don't get it? Dad hated fighting!" said Adam.

"One sure way to turn a man to peace is to have him fight in a war," said Tora. "He told me that Green had planned the Coda Program and that it was he who was supposed to set it in motion when the wars were lost to the dinosaurs. Marcus Green could not imagine a world where humans and dinosaurs lived side by side, but your father could."

"So he built Bastion,"

said Chloe. She
looked around proudly at her
home, the sanctuary that her
father had made.

They were all silent for a few
moments.

"When we found the bunker, the
computer mistook me for Dad. The
Coda Program has been started. We
have four weeks," said Adam, looking
down at his feet. Tora's eyes widened.

"Then we must stop it," she said.

"But how?" said Adam. "All we've got is this
stupid manual and it's full of technical mumbo-
jumbo! We can't understand a word of it!" He
threw it down to the ground in frustration where
it made a thud in the red dust. Dag picked it up
and opened it.

"Ha!" barked Dag. Everyone looked over to
him, where he was

reading the manual. He looked up at the blank faces staring at him. "Sorry, it's just funny. They've written in here that you need an electromagnet with a power of X multiplied by Y, but they should have written X multiplied by Z squared." More blank faces. "It's, er, funny if you like electromagnets, I guess."

"Dag, can you understand that manual?" asked Chloe.

"Yeah, of course. Pretty simple stuff really. You just need four crystals to activate the disarmament. I'm not sure what sort of crystals though."

Tora laughed and walked off, thudding her way across the red, dusty land.

"Follow me!" she called. Dag and the group of humans ran to catch up.

*

In the centre of Bastion was a metal hut that

was locked shut. It had wires extending out of it leading to all parts of the settlement, providing power to help grow crops and give light. It was the only source of electricity in Bastion but Adam realised that he had no idea how it generated the power. He never really thought about stuff like that – he left that to Dag.

"Of course!" said Dag, as he approached the hut. Tora had reached the hut quickly and had stood waiting for the rest of them. "The Dilotron crystal!"

"The – *puff* – what?" asked Adam, running to keep up.

"All our electricity comes from one place. The Dilotron crystal!"

Adam looked breathless and confused. He shrugged, as if to say 'I haven't a clue what you're talking about'.

"Dilotron? It was discovered by humans and is a completely clean energy," said Dag. "The crystal emits power and it lasts forever. If we had four crystals we could get enough power to shut down the Coda Program. We'd have to go directly to the weapons lab of course and find three other crystals..."

"Why *four* crystals?" asked Adam. Dag quickly looked back into the manual.

"Um, I saw it here somewhere... ah, here it is! *'The four crystals will, when placed in the disarmament chamber, create a Quadri-Dilotron reaction that will cause the spores to become deactivated',*" said Dag.

"I'm so glad I asked," said Adam, still none the wiser.

"It'll be like boiling a baby's bottle to kill the germs," translated Chloe.

Dag used his strong claw to break open the lock on the door to the hut. The door flew open revealing a mess of wires and circuits. He looked over to Tora. "Can I, um, take this?"

Tora nodded.

"It is for the greater good, after all," she said. "Just make sure you bring it back!"

He reached in and grabbed something. There was a bang, some sparks and then silence as the electricity across Bastion died. Dag pulled his hand from the hut and Adam saw that he was holding a yellow crystal, about the size of an apple. It shone and glimmered in the light of the sun. Dag offered it to Adam. Adam nervously took the crystal from Dag.

"It's so small," he said. "And there are others like this?"

Tora nodded.

"As far as we know, every settlement has one," said Tora. "If you are to stop the Coda Program from destroying every dinosaur on the planet, you will need to collect three more."

Adam cradled the crystal in his hand. He knew he had to go. It was he who had –

accidentally – started all this. If he didn't he would doom all dinosaurs to extinction... again. And all because he wanted to see what was behind that stupid door. He turned to Chloe.

"It's my mistake. I have to make it right," he said. "I have to go and stop the Coda Program. But I can't leave you here alone."

"I'll make it easy for you then," said Chloe, taking his hand. "I'm coming with you."

"And I'm coming too," said Dag. "There's no point arguing. I'm the only one that can understand the manual, so you need me."

"And us!" shouted Benji and Tuppence. They jumped up and down in excitement.

"No," came the stern reply from Tora. Her voice boomed across Bastion. "You are far too young and would be too much of a distraction to the main quest."

"So it's a *quest* now, is it?" muttered Adam. He looked down at the crystal in his hand and then over to the rest of Bastion. It was his home, where he was born and raised. The thought of leaving made him feel sick to his stomach. Worse still was the thought that he may not even make it back.

Looking back to Dag, Chloe, Tora and the twins, he knew the decision was already made for him. If he did not go searching for the crystals, he would lose not just his home, but his family as well.

"Looks like we're all crewed up," he said with a nervous smile. "When do we leave?"

Chapter Four.

They prepared to leave immediately. Adam would have preferred a while longer at home to ready himself for the journey ahead, but the countdown had already begun. Time was against them.

"Pack light," said Chloe as they returned to their hut. It was messy, as always, which was how Adam left it every morning. Resisting the urge to put everything back in its place, Chloe grabbed a small cloth bag and filled it with a loaf of bread, some pots of nuts and berries, and a length of bandage. "Just in case," she muttered to herself.

Adam simply took his jacket and filled his pockets with bits of food he could find. He was about to leave when he trod on something small and springy. He bent down to pick up a bouncy ball, about as big as a peach, made from hundreds of tiny rubber bands stretched around themselves.

It had been his father's. Adam had a few memories of his dad, but the one that stood out was of him pacing the floor, thinking and muttering, planning how to build and manage the settlement of Bastion. He would bounce the ball on the floor as he paced, a playful act to focus his mind. Adam closed his hand around the ball and thought about the thousands of hours that it had taken his father to establish the peaceful enclave of Bastion.

He thought of the amount of times that ball had been bounced in tension and stress. And he thought about how in four weeks it could all be for nothing, just because Marcus Green had believed that peace between humans and dinosaurs was impossible.

"We'll stop it, Dad. For you," he whispered, and pocketed the ball.

Adam and Chloe walked back to the outskirts of Bastion, where a fence made of scrap metal, old broken cars and junk served as the barrier between them and the rest of New Earth. The gates had been welded by their mother and had not been opened in years. The last time someone had entered Bastion had been when a herd of stegosauri had arrived looking for protection. No one, however, had ever *left* the settlement.

"It is a great thing you are doing," said Tora. She had waited by the gates and a crowd had amassed. They were certain something was going on as it was rare that Tora ever left her cave. "We have gathered some supplies for you." A young boy trotted forward and handed a bag of food to Adam, who thanked him.

"We'll be back soon," he said, looking up to Tora. "I promise."

"Where are the twins?" Chloe asked.

"They went off in a temper after I would not let them join you," said Tora. "I know they would wish you well."

Adam hopped from one foot to another, butterflies performing a ballet in his tummy. He had never left Bastion but was keen to get moving and start the journey. He was restless and squeezed the rubber ball in his pocket to relieve his tension.

"Where has Dag got to?" he snapped. "We can't go without him."

Tora lifted her head high above the crowd of assembled humans and dinosaurs and saw the figure of Dag approaching.

"Here he is," she said, and her eyes widened in disbelief. "What on New Earth...?"

The crowd parted to let Dag through. Before he could see him, Adam could hear a clanking and scraping of metal. He turned to see Dag dressed from head to claw in metal with gadgets and inventions attached. On his rear was a tail-mounted grappling hook, his sides carried saddlebags full of gizmos and sat on his back like a knight on his horse was a self-lighting portable gas stove that he had been working on. Even on his front legs he wore silver pads which held some sort of electronic circuitry. Adam and Chloe burst out laughing.

"What have you come as?" said Adam. "Robo-Dag?"

The crowd around them tittered. Dag looked down at the ground, his cheeks reddening.

"I thought we'd need some of my inventions," he shrugged.

"Where exactly are we going?" said Adam, the thought finally hitting him. "How are we supposed to find the other crystals?" Tora bent down to them.

"Bastion is not the only settlement on New Earth," she said. "After the wars, cities began to form all over the land. Each was filled with a different species of dinosaur. Ours is the only one to contain different dinos and certainly the only one with humans that I know of. It is likely each city has its own source of power at its centre."

Adam gulped. So out there, somewhere, were cities filled with dinosaurs. And the future of New Earth depended on him, his little sister and a techno-clad iguanodon finding a Dilotron crystal at the heart of them.

"So we get into the cities, get the crystals and

get out?" he confirmed. He was so nervous his teeth were nearly chattering.

"And then the sticky business of disarming the laboratory, before it releases the killer spores into the world," said Dag. Chloe flashed a worried look at him. "Which should be easy-peasy, according to this!" He raised his manual and gave Chloe what was supposed to be a reassuring smile.

"I packed a map," said Chloe. "The nearest city is a few days walk away. I suggest we start now."

"Wait!" said Tora. She lowered her massive head down to Adam. In her teeth she held a necklace and Adam's arms sagged under its weight as he took it. "This is for you. To keep Bastion forever in your thoughts." The necklace was long and heavy and held a crest at the centre; the symbol of Bastion, a human and dinosaur side-by-side. "Your mother made it.

She made one for each of the founders of this settlement."

Adam could not speak. He was touched at the gesture, but also rigid with fear. The necklace had been made for Tora, who was around twenty times his size. He found though that he could wrap the necklace around his waist twice to make a cool-looking belt. He nodded to the gate, which was pulled open by two apatasauruses with chains around their necks. With a glance to his sister, Adam stepped forward out of the gates and into the land beyond.

As the three friends left their home, the sound of applause and cheers came from the humans of Bastion, while the dinosaurs cheered in the only way they knew how. Each dinosaur lifted its head to the sky and howled, deep and long, so that soon a long drone echoed off the stone walls of the gorge.

The first part of the journey kept them all

silent for some time, climbing the wall of the gorge using the steps that the Human Army had carved into them years ago. They all concentrated, huffing and puffing as they climbed the sloping rockface.

After a few hours they made it to the top and found themselves in a large wood. The trees were old and thick, making a natural curtain which hid the gorge from the outside, making Bastion hard to find.

They walked in silence for some time, Chloe only occasionally pausing to check the map and point the way. The sound of Dag's machinery and the soft thud of his large feet on the ground beneath was the only noise. An hour in, Adam broke the silence.

"So... we're on a quest to save the world?" he asked.

"Yup," said Dag.

"Just your average Tuesday then..."

They all laughed, long and hard. It was a
laugh born out of tension and nervousness,
where the only other way of releasing their
emotions would be to scream or cry.
Chloe wiped the tears of laughter from
her eyes.

"We should probably discuss how we're going to do this. Do we even have a plan?" she said, trying to regain her calm.

"Here's a plan," said Adam. "The crystals are in the city. We break into the city, attack the centre, take the crystals and run. What do you think?" Chloe snorted.

"I think you've been reading too many adventure books from the library," said Chloe. "Attack the centre? What with? We're not an army, Adam."

Adam pouted. Even on an adventure to save the earth, he had his little sister arguing with him.

"I hate to admit it Adam, but she's right. We don't have the weaponry to go in all guns blazing," said Dag.

"What weaponry do we have?" asked Adam.

"Er... none," said Dag, feeling foolish. "Bastion is a peaceful settlement. There were no weapons, unless you count mousetraps. What *I* thought we could do was break into the dino-cities, use stealth tactics to sneak into the main power hub, disconnect the Dilotron crystal and then get out of there."

Chloe sighed.

"Dag, you're two-metre high dino dressed in metal sheeting. How did you plan on being stealthy?" she laughed. Now it was Dag's turn to sulk.

"What's your big idea then?" he snapped. Snapping wasn't in his nature, so he immediately followed it up with a meek "sorry..."

"I think we should be up front with them," said Chloe. "Go to the front gate, ask to speak to their leader and explain the whole end-of-the-world-as-we-know-it thing. I'm sure once they know how it will help save them, they will just hand the crystal over to us." Chloe looked smug but Adam wasn't convinced.

"So you want to go up to a giant carnivorous dino, its jaws dripping with juice from its last victim, and reason with it?" said Adam. "Fine, go ahead. But don't come running to me when he bites your legs off..."

With all three of them in a bad mood, the silence returned.

Another two hours in, their silence was broken by a small yelp.

"What was that?" whispered Dag. They stopped. They were on a dirt track, lined on each side by tall trees.

"I don't know," said Adam. He picked up a rock and prepared to throw it. "Arm yourself!"

"Wait!" said Chloe. "It could be anything! A friend, or a gust of wind! You can't just attack anything that moves, Adam."

Suddenly the same yelp came from the trees to the left and Dag screamed, running out of the way. Adam, rock still in hand, leapt to the tree

and parted the leaves with one hand, ready to
strike a blow with the other.

"Stop!" The small figures of Benji and
Tuppence stood with their hands in the air. Their
faces were almost unrecognisable with dirt and
leaves stuck out of their curly brown hair.
Tuppence picked a thorny branch out of her arm.

"Surprise!" cheered Benji.

"I take it back," said Chloe, shaking her head
in disbelief. "Adam, attack."

"No, wait!" shouted Tuppence. "We just
thought you'd need some help on the way.
Lookouts and stuff."

"So you followed us all the way out into the
wild? What if you'd been in an accident? Tora
didn't know where you were,
neither did we!" said
Adam, his face red.

"That's the beauty
of being a twin,

innit?" said Benji. "Always travel in pairs."

"Tora told you not to come," said Chloe. "She's going to kill you if you go back."

"All the more reason to let us stay with you," smiled Tuppence. Adam sighed.

"They *were* stealthy," said Dag. "It might be good to have a couple of foot soldiers."

Adam looked at Chloe, who shrugged.

"Fine," said Adam. "Looks like we're the babysitters now, as well as the defenders of the planet!"

Chapter Five.

The darkness closed in on them and they slept through the night, a campfire burning between them to keep them warm. When they woke, they set off almost immediately, aware that they still had far to go.

Benji and Tuppence joined them, walking ahead and poking their heads around corners.

"All clear, Captain!" shouted Benji. Adam played along, saluting them. It took them most of the day to get through the forest, but by evening they reached the edge and found themselves on a dry scrubland that seemed to stretch on forever. The twins took the chance to run without the risk of bashing into a tree every few metres, whooping and cheering. They came to the brow of a hill and stopped. "Woah..."

Adam and Chloe raced ahead to see what was the matter (Dag, loaded with gadgets, took a while longer). As they approached the top of the hill they saw what had amazed the twins.

Below them, a few miles in the distance, was an enormous dino-city. Easily twice the size of Bastion, it had a tall city wall that circled it, a sprawling network of dwellings and at the centre, a massive tower that rose into the sky like a shard of glass.

"What... is... *that*?" said Adam, unable to wrap his mind around the size of it.

"That, my dear brother," said Chloe, "is Raptor City."

Overwhelmed at the sight of their first target, Adam suggested that they stop for food. Rolling out a blanket, they sat in a circle on the ground and tucked into the food they had brought.

"Um... could you spare a bite or two for some poor orphans?" asked Tuppence. She flashed a sweet smile. Adam rolled his eyes and threw them a roll of bread each and some vegetables.

"So you hike out into the middle of nowhere and you didn't think to bring enough food?" he said.

"This has to last us the entire journey you know. We can't just live off the land."

"Speak for yourself," said Dag. He was chewing on a branch that he had picked further down the path. Chloe laid out the map in the centre of their huddle.

"This is Raptor City, the closest settlement to Bastion," she said, pointing. "Once we're done here we need to move on to these two cities. Then find the right place to disarm the Coda Program."

"According to the manual, we have to get to a place called Brizaul. It's in the West," said Dag. "But first, we've got to survive the raptors."

Nerves got to Adam again and he put down his bread, appetite gone.

"What do we know about the city?" he asked. "I'm guessing it's full of raptors, but what kind?"

"Unfortunately it's not the fluffy kind that like cuddles and rainbows," Dag joked. "Seriously, we know there are velociraptors, utahraptors, pyroraptors..."

"Cool!" said Benji. "Let's go and see!"

Chloe pulled him back to the ground as he tried to run toward the city.

"Not cool!" she said. "Very dangerous! There will be thousands of raptors in there. They hunt in packs usually and it would only take one slice of their claws to cut you in two."

"Says the person who wants to reason with them..." said Adam. Chloe blushed.

"Okay, I'm going off my idea..."

With their supper complete, they sat back and watched the sun dipping towards the horizon. Tuppence and Benji watched the city.

"They have four guards on the main gate," said Tuppence. "We'd be best to enter by the east gate, where there are just two." Adam nodded, impressed.

"Now you're earning your food," he said. "Dag, pass me the bread rolls."

Dag searched the floor in front of him.

"There's no food left. You ate it all," he said. Adam looked back into the bag of food.

"There were definitely six rolls," he said. "We've all had one, except Dag. There should be two leftover."

"There's some cheese missing too," said Chloe. She looked over to the twins.

"What?" said Benji, offended. "Why would we take it? We can just ask you for it!"

"You always accuse us!" said Tuppence. "Like that time those corn cobs went missing back in Bastion."

"That *was* you," said Chloe. Tuppence thought.

"Oh, yeah. I forgot about that," she mumbled. "Still, it weren't us this time."

Dag shushed them all. He signalled to the bushes at the side of the road and took an apple from the bag. Silently he placed it on the floor.

"Dag, what are you–" Adam began. Dag silenced him with a look and pressed his clawed finger to his lips. He then fished around in one of the saddlebags that hung from his back and placed a mirror on the blanket near the food. He also held a small mirror in his hand. He sat facing the city on the horizon.

"Beautiful sunset, hmm?" he said, nodding for the rest of them to do the same. They played along, each a little wary that Dag may have gone crazy. Once they were all facing away from the apple, Dag angled his mirror so that he could see it in the reflection. The mirror placed nearby also helped him to see the back of the fruit. Adam kept one eye on Dag as he faced the sunset. Once he saw what Dag was up to, he played along.

"Yeah, amazing sunset..."

Just then there was a slight rustling from the bushes. Dag did his best not to turn around until he could see in the mirror what he was dealing with. He turned the mirror slightly and took a sharp intake of breath.

"NOW!" he yelled. Adam and Dag span around and dived for the thief. It was a short dinosaur with small arms and brownish-red scales, around the size of a large chicken. It hissed as Adam grabbed its tail and whipped around, attempting to bite him with its sharp canine teeth. It missed, but Adam let go anyway. He didn't want to lose a hand for the sake of an apple.

Dag had missed on his first dive, but managed to grab it on the second. It struggled but he held firm. It let out a high pitched squeal and Dag heard more rustling from the bushes.

"Dag, watch out!" called Adam from the floor, but it happened too fast. Three more small dinosaurs, the same colour and size, burst out of the bushes and set upon Dag. Dag screamed as

they attempted to gnaw his legs, but he was
protected by the metal strapped to him.

"STOP!" barked one of the small dinosaurs.

"DROP!" said another.

Dag let go of the dinosaur in his hands and
they all stopped attacking him.

"Ugh! Just our luck. Lycorhinuses," Dag said, brushing himself down.

"Oh, they're sweet!" said Chloe, bending down to their level. "Are you alright?"

"Yeah, I'll be fine," said Dag.

"I was talking to *them*," said Chloe. She picked up the apple and offered it to them. One bent forward and snatched it, backing away instantly. "You're hungry, aren't you?"

The lycorhinuses eyed Chloe suspiciously. They spoke in single words, barking them at her.

"NEED!"
"FOOD!"
"MUM!"
"GONE!"

They devoured the apple.

"Orphans," said Benji. "Like us."

"They're cute!" said Tuppence. "Can we keep them?"

"Keep them? They're not pets! They're dim-witted little scavengers," said Dag.

"Hey!" said Adam.

"It's true! Too stupid to form their own settlement. After the war they just lived in nests like they always had, roaming the scrublands for food. They can't even put a sentence together."

The four lycos growled and hissed at Dag.

"I think I can guess what they're saying," said Tuppence. "And they seem to understand *you* well enough."

"Maybe they can help," said Benji. "They must live around here. Maybe they know how to get into the city."

"YES!" barked one of the lycos.

"Is that true?" said Chloe. "You can get us in?"

The group of lycos leapt up and down in a dance of happiness.

"That's a yes!" said Tuppence. "What do you say, Adam?"

Adam bent down to them, looking them in the eyes.

"Can you do that? If you work with us and help us in our quest, we can give you food and protection."

The lycos looked at each other.

"MUM?" said one, with a quizzical tilt of the head.

"Yes," laughed Chloe. "We'll be your mum."

The lycos appeared to smile.

"YES!"
"LIKE!"
"WORK!"
"FOOD!"

"Just keep them away from me,"

said Dag, sulking over one of the
cuts he had got in the attack. Chloe
brought out a bandage and wrapped it
gently around his arm.

"They're orphans, Dag. Like us. If we
can protect them, we should," she said. Dag
shrugged.

"Okay. Are they even clever enough to have
named themselves?

"GRAK."
"TREK."
"KARP."
"HART."

The twins led them down
the path and played with
the tiny beasts. They
seemed to understand
each other well. Chloe
and Adam looked on.

"We seem to have a full platoon of foot soldiers now," said Adam. "Do you think we did the right thing?"

"I couldn't have left them alone out here," said Chloe. "Besides, they'll keep the twins busy. So, what's the plan?"

Adam was quiet for some time. The truth was, he didn't *have* a plan. While he had visions of storming the city, he knew that the reality would be more brutal. He was nervous, and Chloe was probably the only one who could see it.

"We wait until the sun is fully down and head to the east gate when it's dark. If we're going to sneak into a city full of carnivorous dinos, I really don't want to be seen."

Chapter Six.

The sun had dipped below the horizon and the moon was slowly edging its way across the sky. Adam was gathering his belongings, placing them in the pockets of his jacket and readying himself to enter Raptor City.

"It'll be fine," he muttered, trying to convince himself. "In and out, no trouble." He looked at the rest of his crew, silent with nerves. As the leader, he knew he should say something to inspire them, but nothing came out.

Boom... boom... boom...

The sound came from over the brow of the hill.

"Very funny, guys," said Adam. "Who made that noise?"

The children looked around.

"Not us, Ad," said Dag. It couldn't have been. All of Adam's friends were in front of him. He gulped and despite the cool evening, began to sweat.

Boom, boom, boom...

"Friend of yours?" he asked the little lycorhinuses. They too began to quake on the spot.

"NO!"
"BIG!"
"CHOMPER!"
"HIDE!"

Adam went cold with terror.

BOOM!

The sound was getting closer!

"Hide! Everyone, GO!" said Chloe in a raised

whisper. Tuppence, Benji and the lycos did not need telling twice. They scattered, diving into bushes. Dag, Chloe and Adam however, being bigger, took a few more moments to find a place.

Chloe crouched behind a tree and Adam found a rock to perch behind. Dag was the last to hide, lying flat on the floor in the open air next to a rock. He was concealed in the shadow, but had to hope that whatever was out there had bad eyesight.

"Everyone be still!" whispered Adam.

BOOM! BOOM! BOOM!

A large dinosaur came lumbering around the corner, its claws thumping on the ground. It was a titanosuchus, a carnivore that hunted alone and had never joined a dino-city. Instead these dinosaurs wandered the scrublands, picking off prey, viciously attacking them with its fang-like canine teeth.

It walked forwards and snuffled at the remains of Chloe's hunk of bread. It tasted some, but spat it out quickly.

It looked up, sniffing the air.

"Humans?" it grunted. "Nah!"

Adam was still behind his rock, but he could see the smaller bushes rocking slightly where the twins and the lycos were.

The titanosuchus plodded forward through their small campsite. He placed his claws down just a pace away from Dag's head. Dag froze.

Chloe was the furthest away from the beast and so waited until its head was turned. She then picked up a nearby rock and threw it as far up the track as she could.

The titanosuchus flinched when the rock landed and sped away to see what had made the noise. Once Chloe could see that it was out of earshot, she gave the all clear.

"Phew! Relax everyone. He's gone!" she said. Dag had turned pale with fear. He stood and brushed himself down.

"Oh good," he said, "just the city full of raptors to deal with now..."

*

From their position at the east of the city, Adam and Chloe carefully picked their way down a hillside. Dag followed behind, with the twins and the lycos easily hopping down the slope. They met at the bottom.

"Okay, there are two lookout towers either side of the gate, staffed by guards," said Dag. He peered through a pair of binoculars he had brought with him, flicking from day to night vision mode. Two figures were now visible in the tops of the towers. "They have weapons. Pulse blasters by the looks of it. Any questions?"

"I've got one," said Adam. "How come you've got cool night vision binoculars? I've only got a wind up torch!"

"I, um, made them myself from some stuff I found lying around. I'll let you have a go with them if you like..."

"Boys!" sighed Chloe. "Can we try to focus on how to get into the city, rather than what toys you brought along? Do we have a plan?"

"I guess we could try and sneak up and wait

until someone leaves. Then rush inside before the gates shut," said Adam with a shrug. He knew it wasn't a great plan, but it was better than nothing.

"We'd never all get through before the gates shut," said Chloe. "Why can't we just go and ask to be let in?"

"Because raptors aren't known for their manners," said Dag. "I could try to open the gates by re-wiring the circuits, but I'd need time. Perhaps if we–"

Benji sighed and Tuppence rolled her eyes. They signalled to each other to move and set off in the direction of the gate. Under the cover of darkness they ran ahead, keeping low. The lycos squeaked and followed them, barging past Adam, who was still arguing with Chloe and Dag.

"Hey!" Adam whispered. "Come back!" The lycos ignored him, concerned only for their new friends, the twins. "Benji! Tuppence! Where do you think you're going?"

Benji turned and pressed his finger to his lips, then pointed to the gate.

Adam could only watch as the children ran towards the dino-city. They reached the towers, Benji under one, Tuppence under the other. The lycos still remained further back, waiting to see what they were required to do. Thankfully the raptors had not thought to use searchlights, so the only lights came from the burning torches at the top of the towers where the guards stood.

With a nod to each other, Benji and Tuppence started to climb their tower. They were good at this, having helped with harvesting fruits from the orchard trees every summer since they could walk. They scaled the towers easily and waited with their heads just below the parapets, just metres away from the raptor guards.

"Be careful..." Adam muttered under his

breath. Chloe realised she hadn't breathed in a full minute.

Positioning themselves on the inside of the towers, Benji and Tuppence managed to glance at each other. They were clinging on to the stonework whilst eight metres above the ground and ten metres apart. They each gave another nod, then popped their head above the wall at the same time.

"Boo!" they each yelled, startling the guards. The raptors span and, seeing the human heads grinning at them from the tower wall, each reached for their weapons. The pulse blasters were small, handheld weapons but packed a punch. They turned and pointed their guns at where Benji and Tuppence had been, but the twins had since dropped to the ground. The guards pressed their triggers anyway, firing a pulse blast directly at each other. The pulse beams passed in mid-air and rammed into the other raptor guard, knocking each other out cold.

On the ground, the twins brushed themselves off. Adam, Chloe and Dag walked up to the gate.

"Impressive," said Dag. "Crazy, but impressive. Now let's re-wire the gate mechanism..."

"NO!" barked Grak. He seemed to whistle to the other lycos who immediately jumped up and piled on each other's backs, making a three-dinosaur high tower. Grak leapt on top and the tower unsteadily made his way to a panel in the gate. Grak jabbed at it with his sharp beak and the cover flew off. He jabbed again and sparks flew from the circuitry inside. With a whirr and a click, the gates started to open.

"Who's the dim-witted little scavengers now then?" said Benji, as he walked past Dag.

Beyond the gates was Raptor City.

Slowly, Adam and Chloe moved through the entrance and into the city. It was not what they had been expecting. As most of the technology to build cities had been destroyed in the Dino Wars, Adam's home town of Bastion was crudely built, using ancient techniques such as mud bricks and straw to make their huts. It looked as though the raptors had it even worse. As far as they could see, the dwellings had been made out of old bits of rubbish. Old cars had been hollowed out, bits of sheet plastic used as shelters and walls of rubble were used to separate living areas. It was a dinosaur shanty town, where the poorest raptors lived.

"Yikes," whispered Dag, "not the friendliest of places. Or the cleanest."

"Notice anything odd?" said Chloe. She pointed at the street lights that lit the mud tracks between the houses. They too were basic, a simple gas-powered flame above a metal pole.

"No electricity. If they have a Dilotron crystal, why aren't they using it to make light? I thought raptors were meant to be intelligent?"

"They are," said Dag. "Working as a team they can do loads of stuff. They were great warriors in the wars. Something is holding them back."

Tuppence had walked ahead. She looked up at a wall, full of posters.

"I think I know what that 'thing' might be."

The wall was covered in political posters, issuing orders and demands to the citizens of Raptor City. On each, the image of a grinning velociraptor beamed at them. The headlines of the images were chilling.

'LORD STRYKER IS WATCHING!'

'LAST YEAR, LORD STRYKER CARRIED OUT OVER 400 EXECUTIONS – PERSONALLY!'

'RE-ELECT LORD STRYKER FOR

TWENTY MORE YEARS OF SAFETY AND
PROTECTION – OR ELSE!'

"Wow," said Chloe. "Someone likes his own
face a bit too much. I'm guessing Lord Stryker is
their leader?"

Benji ran up to them, having scouted ahead.

"You're not going to believe this!" he said,
running back up the path. They followed.

Ahead in the shanty town, the path opened up
into a square. By daytime it might have been a
market square, buzzing with life. By night-time,
it was sinister and eerie. Their shadows flickered
in the gaslight and in the centre of the square
stood a gigantic bronze sculpture of the same
grinning velociraptor, Lord Stryker.

"Uh-oh..." Adam gulped. "I don't think
reasoning with him is an option anymore,
Chloe."

Forming the base of the sculpture was a tank.
Stryker stood on top of it, stamping on it with

his foot. Dag read the plaque on the bottom.

" *'Lord General Stryker, hero of the Dino Wars, crushes his hated enemies with his superior might. All hail Lord Stryker.'* "

"Look!" said Tuppence. "He's wearing a girly necklace!"

Adam and Dag looked up at the sculpture, which indeed had a necklace on it. Dangling around its neck was what looked like a crystal attached to a chain. The statue's was carved from stone of course, but it looked familiar.

"Do you think that's the Dilotron crystal?" asked Dag. Adam smiled.

"There's only one way to find out," he said. "Ask the man himself."

Chloe joined the whispering boys and shot Adam a glare that could have melted a warship.

"Are you crazy? You want to go and see that... maniac?" she said, her voice rising louder than it should have. She stopped, reminding

herself that she was in the centre of a city full of carnivores.

"Why not? That looks like the crystal we need. If we can get inside his home, we could steal it. Maybe he takes it off when he has a nap or something?" Even to Adam that sounded ridiculous. "Or... something..."

"You don't even know where he lives!" said Chloe.

"Someone who likes that much power? I'd be willing to take a guess," said Adam. He pointed upwards to the huge building in the centre, rising above them, stabbed into the heart of the city. Red lights dotted its windows.

Chloe stood immobile for some time before she relented and followed the rest of them up the mud path that led them to the skyscraper.

Adam was tired. His legs ached and his eyes were heavy. It was hard to believe that he was about to end the day with a walk in a strange city, followed by a jewel heist. He walked on however, aware that if he just gave up and fell asleep on the ground, he would be breakfast for some very surprised raptors in the morning.

He watched as Tuppence and Benji ran between the shanty huts, checking the coast was clear. The lycos comically followed them, zigzagging across the path and peeking around corners. It was Grak, the one with the dappled markings on his back, who seemed to be the leader of the four of them. He was always only a pace behind Benji and had led the group to open the gates. Trek was the fastest, noticeably thinner than the rest. Karp was distinguishable by her chipped canine tooth and orange eyes, while Hart was definitely the runt of the litter. She was forever trying to catch up and had a way of running that was comical, like a drunken chicken. She seemed to be happy enough and the rest of the lycos looked after her. Adam was amazed and pleased at the way that they got on with the twins, like they had been friends for life, not just the day.

The road led uphill and they soon found themselves just a hundred metres from the skyscraper. Around them the snores of raptors came from the shanty huts. They kept their voices low.

"No guard," said Dag, looking through his binoculars again. "There must be an alarm on the door. There's no way they'd build something that big and not have security."

"How are they powering the lights in that thing? It's blinding!" said Adam. Dag just pointed up to the sides of the tower, where silent wind-turbines turned in the darkness. Dag crept forward and approached the door. It was eerie with no one around, like a trap waiting to be sprung. He spotted a panel on the wall next to the door and prised it open with his claw. Inside was a number keypad with a digital display.

"Four numbers to enter. What would a raptor choose as a passcode?" Dag mumbled to himself. Raptors were good hunters in a pack, but on their own they could be quite dim. He attempted the obvious '1234', but the keypad gave him a low rasping sound and the words '2 TRIES LEFT' scrolled across the screen. He gave a shrug to Adam and Chloe, who were waiting in the shadows of the shanty huts. Attempting to stop his shaking hand, he tried '1111' but again he got the rasping sound.

'1 TRY LEFT.'

Dag gulped. He had no clue what to put in. What would happen if he failed? Would the alarm sound? Would the door lock forever?

Adam could see what was happening. What should Dag do? He racked his brains.

"What is the greatest date in raptor history?" Adam whispered to Chloe hurriedly. "What about when they won the war? What year was that?"

Chloe knew the date exactly. She had read all about the Dino Wars in the library in Bastion. She pushed past Adam and ran to Dag at the keypad. He was about to take his last guess when the small figure of Chloe came bounding towards him and barged him out of the way.

"3122!" she said, tapping the numbers in. "The year of the Battle of Raptor Valley. They won against the Allied Human Forces."

She crossed her fingers as the display lingered on the numbers for a second or two longer.

A pleasant beep followed by the unlocking of the door told them that it had worked. Chloe was unable to contain her joy.

"YES!" she yelled, high-fiving Dag. But her voice had been just a tad too loud. They all froze as the snores from the huts stopped. The doors

flung open and they were joined outside by
thirty raptors, all wielding pulse blasters.

"Oops," said Chloe.

Chapter Seven.

"Ow! Watch it!" yelled Benji. An armed utahraptor pushed him through the gleaming white corridors of the skyscraper. "You just knocked me into the wall!"

"We're prisoners, Benji. I think he meant to," said Dag. He was being pushed in the back with a pulse blaster as he walked along, his wrists tied.

"Affirmative," said the guard in a growl of a voice. "Lord Stryker allows us to bash the prisoners about now and again. Just a perk of the job. Now, shut up." He rammed the butt of his blaster into Dag's foot, who let out a howl.

The skyscraper's stairs and corridors were seemingly never-ending. The whole structure had been built by raptors without plans or any expertise. They had simply piled building materials on top of each other until it looked something like a tower. The sloping walls and uneven floors were making Adam dizzy, like walking through a hall of mirrors.

Soon they had arrived at a room with a makeshift jail cell, the bars welded together from scrap metal. It was slapdash, but effective. The door creaked open.

"Get in and pipe down," said the raptor guard. They threw them all in one by one. "Lord Stryker will soon decide what to do with you."

With a slam of the door and a jingle of keys, they were left alone. Or so they thought.

"Ah! Company!" said a voice. Dag jumped and turned to see what he thought had been a pile of junk in the corner rise up to become a small, wiry, elderly raptor.

"Aaagh!" screamed Benji and Tuppence. "He's going to eat us!"

They dived for cover behind Adam and Chloe.

"Relax," said Adam. "I don't think he means us any harm."

The raptor chuckled and placed some spectacles on the end of his snout.

"Really? And what would make you think that, dear boy?" He seemed to smile. Adam already had a feeling of warmth towards him.

"Well, the fact that you're in the same jail as us probably means that you're an enemy of Lord Stryker," said Adam. "Which kind of makes us on the same side, wouldn't you say?"

The raptor clapped his claws in delight.

"Quite so! Deftly worked out, Mr...?"

"Caine. Adam Caine," said Adam, following

it with a round of introductions.

"And they call me Oska. Pleased to meet you," said Oska. "There is of course another reason I did not eat you, apart from the fact that it is well past my mealtime. Anyone else care to guess?"

Dag stepped forward.

"Y-you're an oviraptor," said Dag. "It means 'egg thief'. You eat eggs, not people."

Oska seemed to frown.

"Well, yes, I suppose. It's rubbish of course; my species was misnamed by the humans. I am a carnivore, just like those out there," he said, nodding to the door. "I can eat meat just as well as any raptor. I actually meant that there are nine of you and one of me. I simply could not take you all on. Not that I would!"

Adam went to the door and tried to force it open.

"It won't give, I'm afraid. I've been trying for

two years," said Oska.

"Two years? What are you in for?" asked Chloe.

"Oh, just a little treason!" he said. He had a glint in his eye like an old man with a secret to tell. "I was Stryker's advisor for some time. I simply made some suggestions he didn't like. Such as to step down and give the job to someone who isn't crazy!"

Dag laughed out loud.

"How come he didn't execute you?" he asked.

"Well, I *am* his uncle, so that may have had something to do with it," Oska chuckled. "And what have you done to displease the silly little brat?"

Adam and Chloe shared a glance and Adam nodded. For some reason, he trusted this raptor.

"We're on a mission to save every dinosaur on earth from being killed," said Chloe. Oska chuckled again, but then saw they were deadly serious.

"But... but you're just a bunch of kids!"

"Oska, when did Stryker become leader?" asked Dag. Oska replied that it was around twenty years ago. "Was it around the time that he got hold of a stone like this?"

Adam fished out their own Dilotron crystal.

"Goodness me," said Oska. "It's just like the one on his pendant! What does that mean?"

"It means," said Dag, "that we were right, Adam. The crystal we want is in this building. Unfortunately it is around the neck of the most dangerous dinosaur in the city."

*

They were held for a few hours until the sun started to rise outside their barred window, then taken from the cell and herded by guards with pulse blasters into an open space containing just one large chair. It had been made by welding together piles of old human weapons from the Dino Wars. Rifles were joined to swords and cannons, grenades were fixed onto the outside like decorations. Atop the magnificent metal structure was Stryker himself.

"Crikey," said Adam under his breath. "He's built himself a throne room."

"Silence, human!" barked Stryker. His voice was not the powerful boom that Adam was expecting, but a whiny drawl. High up on his throne, he loomed above them all but he was in fact quite small for a velociraptor. He was thin too. If he was a human he would have been called a weakling. *How is* he *the leader of this city?* Adam thought.

"Face Lord Stryker!" said one of the guards. They all turned, their hands tied in front of them. Adam looked to the floor and caught sight of the long necklace Tora had given him, tied around his waist.

"You break into my city? You assault my guards? You have the nerve to enter my tower, my sanctuary?" said Stryker with disgust in his voice. "Finally you have committed the worst crime of all; being human."

The lycorhinuses each looked up, confused.

"NOT!"
"ME!"

"NOT!"

"ME!" they barked in turn.

"Or me," said Dag. "You probably noticed that though..."

Stryker leapt down from his throne in a single jump. At ground level he wasn't even the same height as Dag. He walked up to Dag and peered at him, like he was some horrid medical specimen.

"Yessss..." he hissed. "And you have been with them every step of the way. Traitors to the Dinosaur Army. If there is one thing I hate more than humans, it is dinos that have turned their back on their own kind and joined scum like *them*." Adam was close to Stryker now and looked straight at him. He could see his black eyes and his flaking, scaled skin. He could also see the chain around his neck which held a glowing, orange jewel. The Dilotron crystal!

"Where did you come from?" Stryker demanded.

Silence. Adam glanced towards Chloe and the twins, who remained quiet. Stryker noted their silence and gave a quick nod to the guard behind Chloe. He saluted his leader and rammed the butt of his blaster into the back of Chloe's knee, making her fall to the ground. He put his blaster to his shoulder and aimed.

"BASTION!" yelled Adam. Seeing Chloe being treated like that had made the words fly out of his mouth. Stryker nodded.

"The herbivore settlement, beyond the great forest? If I had known you had humans living there as well I would have invaded long ago. As it is, a few days march for a bunch of puny herbies hardly seemed worth it," said the raptor leader. He turned and gave what Adam assumed to be a smile. "Is that what *this* is? An invasion?" he laughed. The guards laughed along, although Adam got the impression it was more out of fear of what Stryker might do if they didn't.

Chloe gulped and cleared her throat.

"Chloe, no!" Adam shouted.

"I have to try, Adam!" she said, turning to Stryker. "Lord Stryker. You are wise and powerful. Your bravery on the battlefield is legendary and as a leader you are unmatched." She was doing well. Stryker was almost glowing with pride. "We have come to tell you of a grave danger to you and all of New Earth."

"A threat?" said Stryker. "Are you threatening me?"

"No! No, just trying to help," said Adam, attempting to calm him. "An old weapon from the Dino Wars has been triggered that could kill all dinosaurs on the planet. We are on our way to disarm it, but we need your help."

The guards behind them were looking at each

other, scared to speak up but clearly concerned at the mention of the word 'weapon'. Adam had their attention.

"Help? What do you want from me?" said Stryker, his voice wavering.

"To disarm the weapon we need four Dilotron crystals," said Chloe. She let her eyes rest on the crystal around his neck. "We need *that*."

Stryker's expression changed from curious to furious. He placed his clawed hand over the crystal, protecting it from the eyes in the room that had turned towards him. He recoiled, stepping back to the safety of his throne.

"Never!" he hissed. He shot a look of hatred at Adam and Chloe. "Guards! Take them to the cells! We will hold a full public execution at noon."

Adam braced himself to be hauled away, but

the claw on his shoulder did not come.

"My Lord, what if they are telling the truth?" said the guard that had pushed Benji. "Maybe if we question them more..."

His voice trailed off as he saw the look in Stryker's eyes. Adam saw it too; it was anger, hatred and fear all rolled into one. It was the look of someone about to crack.

"You. You question *me*?" he said, gripping the Dilotron crystal tight in his hand. "Who is your leader?" The guard gulped and quivered.

"Y-You, my Lord."

Stryker leapt down from the throne again and went up to the guard. If they had been the same height, they would have been snout-to-snout. As it was, Stryker was a head shorter but the guard still looked petrified.

"He's the smallest in the room," whispered Adam to Dag. "Why don't they just attack him?"

"I think it's the crystal. It must be leaking out a small amount of Dilotron power. The manual said the orange crystals aren't as stable as our yellow one, but it should still be okay for us to use," whispered Dag. Stryker began to hit and kick the guard, who did nothing to defend himself. "It makes him feel invincible and strong, so the other raptors fear and respect him. It's like a shortcut to being a great leader. If we can get it off him..."

"...then he won't be leader anymore!" whispered Adam. He smiled. At last a plan was forming in his head. Stryker laid a final blow into the guard, who was now on the floor and whimpering.

"I've heard enough! You insult me with your

made-up schemes and excuses. Trespassing is punishable by death. I shall carry out the execution myself. You two urchins! Kneel!"

The other guards in the room forced Tuppence and Benji to their knees. They cast a panicked look over to their friends, while Stryker pulled a giant broadsword down from the wall. Tuppence cried out in fear.

"Adam! Do something!"

Chapter Eight.

"Dag, use your claw!" Adam blurted out. He turned to face his dinosaur friend who used the sharp claw on the outside of his hand to slice easily through the rope that held Adam's hands together. A guard rushed to stop them but Dag span around. He whacked the utahraptor around the face with his long, thick tail and quickly untied Dag's ties for him.

"Stop!" called Stryker, the broadsword now raised above his head. It was clearly too big for him however; his small raptor hands struggling to keep it aloft. Adam saw he only had seconds before the sword came down on the twins.

He pulled the heavy necklace that Tora had given him from around his waist and twirled it above his head, spinning it faster and faster until he let go. He hurled it towards Stryker and the chain wrapped around his legs, binding them together. The Lord of Raptor City swayed for a moment and then fell backwards, safely away from Benji and Tuppence.

Dag had sliced through Chloe's rope also and she went to the twins, undoing the knots around their wrists. Dag turned and prepared to strike another raptor with his tail, while the lycos had wriggled free of their ropes and were gnawing on the tail of a soldier.

Adam had to get the crystal from Stryker but a guard positioned himself between him and the leader. The guard was the largest soldier Adam had seen yet, with a battle scar running down his face. He grunted and smiled menacingly.

"Make your move, human!" said Scarface.

He stretched his claws, the sharp talons glinting in the light. Adam gulped. He was no match for the raptor and he didn't even have a weapon. An idea hit him. A crazy idea, but it was the only one he had. He reached for his pocket and pulled out his dad's old rubber ball, made from hundreds of elastic bands. He had no time to think, but instead just aimed and threw.

His aim was normally good from playing with Dag and he had a strong throw. The ball however sailed past Scarface, who laughed.

"Is that all you have?" he said. "You should– OOF!"

But the ball had gone exactly where Adam had wanted it to. It bounced off the wall behind the guard and flew into the back of his head. The ball was hard enough to cause some pain and disorientate Scarface. He staggered to the side and Adam saw his chance. He ran, pushing the guard over and diving towards Stryker.

"Get him, you fools!" ordered Stryker. It was too late. Adam reached for the Dilotron crystal and grabbed it, wrenching it free from the velociraptor's neck.

"Noooooo!" yelled Stryker. His neck now bare, his power robbed from him, he turned to the guards who had all frozen at the sound of his pathetic scream. It was as if they had all suddenly lost interest in what they were doing. One guard looked down at his pulse blaster with a frown and dropped it to the floor. Another was about to throw a punch at Dag but he relaxed his fist and stood up straight, much to Dag's relief.

Adam stood and unwrapped his own necklace from Stryker's legs, who leapt up and started to yell.

"Get them!" screamed Stryker. "Destroy them you idiots! What are you waiting for?"

The guards walked over to Stryker, smaller and weaker than all of them. They passed Chloe and the twins, seemingly uninterested in them.

One spoke: "Twenty years you've been leader. Twenty years you treated Raptor City like it was a toy that you could throw away when you got bored. We've lived in fear and in tiny, filthy homes while you lived in a palace. Well, not anymore..."

Stryker cowered. He looked to his side where the broadsword lay and took it by the handle. But without the crystal around his neck giving him power, he could barely manage to lift it from the floor. He dropped it and began to shake as the guards closed in on him.

"Not so high and mighty without this, are you?" Adam said, waving the Dilotron crystal at him. He called to his friends. "Let's get out of here!"

The group ran out, one by one. Adam scooped up his father's rubber band ball and made sure all his friends were clear from the room before he headed out of the door. He cast a quick look back where Stryker was cowering in a corner, surrounded by angry raptors.

Trying to escape the tower was difficult too. They ran down corridors and through rooms but ended up back where they started.

"This is hopeless!" said Chloe. "How are we meant to get out?" Adam saw a door he recognised and realised what he needed to do. Bursting through it, he found the jail and Oska the oviraptor, calmly sitting and meditating.

"Fancy getting out of here?" smiled Adam.

"I thought you'd never ask!" chuckled the old raptor. They took the keys to the cell which had been discarded by a guard and let him out, where he kissed the ground and shook hands with them all. "Right then – escape!"

They ran through the maze of corridors and emerged into the entrance area of the tower.

"What now?" said Chloe, gasping for breath.

"We get out of here," said Adam, stowing the Dilotron crystal in his jacket pocket next to the yellow one from Bastion. "And carefully."

"Now that nasty raptor's not in charge, they won't be after us, will they? We freed them!" said Benji.

"Perhaps we did, but we're still in the centre of a city of carnivores. Ones that haven't seen a tasty human in many years..." said Dag. He glanced to Adam and Chloe, who gulped with fear.

"Let's just get to the gate, slowly and

steadily," said Adam, pushing open the door.

"This way," said Oska, leading them down a side street.

They left the tower and stepped forward into the shanty town. It was morning now, the sun starting to peek past Stryker's tower, but they stuck to the narrow streets and the shadows.

The only sounds to be heard were the faint screams of Stryker above them, but otherwise the dinosaurs of Raptor City were still snug in their beds, not yet awoken. The team of friends walked forwards, tiptoeing as lightly as they could. They had made it this far, but now they had to make it out alive.

Silently they walked down the hill towards the gate they had entered. Adam was feeling good. They had nearly done it. He placed his hand on his jacket pocket and felt the outline of two lumps which proved he had the crystals he needed. Just two more to go.

They reached a ridge and the gate was visible now. It was all Adam could do not to break into a sprint and escape Raptor City forever.

"The gates are still open," he whispered. "We just need to make it there without–"

A loud sound came from behind them. Adam turned to see Dag - his tail had accidently struck a metal lamp post and the sound rang out like a dinner gong.

Slowly, doors of the shanty huts began to open. One by one, the bleary-eyed raptors emerged and started to lick their lips when they saw the escaped humans.

"I think it's time we hit the road," said Chloe. "RUN!"

They set off at a sprint towards the gates but the hordes of raptors gave chase. One of the dinosaurs let out a loud, primal roar and the others followed. Adam didn't dare look back to see how far behind the pack were but kept his

eyes on the gates, their only chance to get out alive.

"Uh-oh!" he shouted. "The gates! They're closing!"

Guards were winding the mechanism to pull the two doors shut. The gates creaked and strained, slowly closing in on each other.

"Run!" yelled Chloe. "We can make it through the gap!"

The group gave an extra burst of speed. Oska was first through the gate and the lycos, being small and fast, were next. Benji and Tuppence followed. Dag reached the gate and tried to hold the doors open. While he was strong, he was still small and he wouldn't be able to hold them for long.

"Chloe, go!" he said. Chloe dived to the ground and slipped under Dag's legs. "Adam! Hurry!"

Adam was the last to reach the gate. He

looked back at the approaching hordes of dinosaurs. Even if he made it through the gate, it would only take a second for them to open it again and then they'd be chased through the scrublands by vicious velociraptors. He had an idea.

"Hold the gate a few seconds longer!" he said to Dag, who was shaking with the effort of keeping the two huge doors apart. Adam dived through his legs to the other side and grabbed one of the large pieces of junk that Dag had insisted on bringing with him. He unhooked it from Dag's backpack and flicked a few switches on it.

"Hey! That's my self-lighting portable gas stove! It's only experimental. It might not work!" Dag yelled above the increasingly deafening sound of screaming raptors. Adam placed it on the ground between the doors.

"It's alright, I'm not planning on cooking

some steak!" Adam said. "Let go now!"

Dag leapt out of the way and the gates slammed shut on the small stove. It was about the size of a large pumpkin but the doors crushed it as they closed. It held the doors open a small amount, enough for a pyroraptor to stick its head through and yell at them. Others tried to climb through, their razor-sharp claws slashing the air.

"Hey, if the gas leaks from that stove and catches fire, it might–" Dag began to say. His face dropped in realisation.

"Let's keep running, shall we?" said Adam with a smile.

Dag was already sprinting away as fast as his scaly legs could carry him. Adam chased after him.

BOOOOM!

The force of the explosion sent Dag and
Adam flying through the air. They landed with a
thud on the ground and looked back to see the
gates on fire. Thanks to the poor building of the
raptors, one of the towers had come loose and
toppled down over the gates.

"That'll take some clearing up," said Adam.
He started to laugh and Dag joined in until they
were both giggling uncontrollably into the night
air.

Chapter Nine.

The sun was rising slowly over the horizon as Adam, Chloe, Dag, Oska, the twins and the lycos climbed up a hill and came to rest on a plateau. The twins collapsed on the ground at once, tired from running away from Raptor City and being up all night. No one had slept since the previous morning and not properly since before they had opened that steel door in the cliff and changed their lives forever. The lycos sat down next to them and snuggled up like they were the family pets.

Adam, Chloe, Oska and Dag stood at the ridge of the hill. They were high above Raptor

City now and as the light came up they could see the chaos that was ensuing inside the city walls. The dinosaurs inside had given up trying to open the gates and chase them and had instead turned on the tower in the centre of the city. Stryker's sky-high palace was being taken apart, brick by brick. The raptors had wasted no time in getting the building materials from the tower and using them to build better shelters for themselves, instead of the rickety shanty houses they called homes.

"Woah," said Dag. "We really messed up their city."

"It was messed up before you got there," said Oska. "Stryker had us all living in fear."

"At least now they have a chance to build their own city the way they want it," said Chloe.

"Everyone should have a right to freedom," said Adam. "Even vicious, flesh-hungry raptors. No offence, Oska."

"None taken, dear boy," said the aging oviraptor. "Would you mind if I tagged along for a while? I fear I'm not welcome back at Raptor City and I would dearly love to see some more of the world. Especially if this virus-weapon-thingy is going to kill us all anyway."

"It won't if I've got anything to do with it," said Adam. "And you're very welcome, Oska. I have a feeling you'll be a useful member of the team."

They surveyed the land around the city from their high vantage point and saw no escaped raptors coming after them.

"We should rest," said Chloe. "Guys, find some shade and get some sleep. Benji, Tuppence, why don't you–"

But the twins were already snoring, the lycos curled up against them. Oska too had settled down for a rest. Chloe smiled.

Dag sat down on the ridge, looking out across

the scrublands and the remains of the city. Adam sat next to him.

"What's up?"

"I made that stove myself, you know," Dag said, sulkily. "It would have been great to have on our journey."

"Is that what you're pouting about?" Adam laughed. He put his arm around his friend's long neck. "I'm sorry I wrecked your invention. You've got to admit though, it made a great firework show!"

Dag smiled. Chloe sat down next to the two boys.

"Can I suggest we go into the next settlement a bit more carefully? Maybe even with a plan?"

"Plan? No way!" said Adam. "Where's the excitement in that? Chloe, I think I've finally found what I was born to do. All those years growing crops in Bastion, I was bored. Now I've finally got a life full of adventure! We can easily get the next crystal. All we have to do is think on our feet and trust our instincts."

"My instincts are telling me to sleep," said Dag.

"Hey, we have crystals to get!" said Adam, shaking Dag to wake him up. "Where is the next city anyway?"

Chloe looked at her map and raised her arm, pointing to a mountain in the distance. Adam grabbed Dag's binoculars and peered through them. All he could make out was a city perched on the side of the mountain, high above the ground. There was no visible track to get there and Adam soon realised why. Flying high above the city were large dinosaurs with massive wingspans and long, pointed beaks with sharp, needle-like teeth.

Pterosaurs.

"Um, maybe we should have a plan after all. You know, just in case," he conceded. He turned to his sister and friend, but they had already lay themselves down on the ground and were sleeping peacefully. Adam smiled and joined them, closing his eyes and dreaming of adventures to come.

Dino Wars will return with

THE TRIALS
OF TERROR

Turn over for a sneaky preview!

"Twenty-three green bottles hanging on a wall… twenty-three green bottles hanging on a wall…"

Adam puffed as he walked up the narrow mountain path. The ground underfoot was rocky and the slightest misjudged step could spell disaster. He had to concentrate each time he placed his feet down or he could easily find himself sliding down the mountainside. The mountain itself was man-made, comprising of the rubbish and junk of a thousand years of waste. Adam remembered his dad telling him that they used to bury rubbish in the ground but when that filled up, they kept piling it up high, until they needed flying machines to dump more on the top. After that, they dumped rock and gravel over it, called it a mountain and pretended that it was their plan all along. Adam found it easier not to speak. Instead he focused on his breathing; the higher up they got, the thinner the air became and the harder it was to take in a breath. *Goodness knows how Benji and Tuppence manage to keep singing*, he thought. He wouldn't have minded their cheerful tunes if they hadn't chosen to start with nine hundred and ninety-nine green bottles…

"And if one green bottle… should accidentally fall… (puff, puff, gasp!)… there'll be twenty-two green bottles hanging on a wall!" The twins sang happily, their curly brown hair bobbing along. Behind them, four tiny dinosaurs trotted along on their chicken-like legs. They followed the twins wherever they went and were similarly unaffected by the walk that the group had been on for nearly two days now. The lycorhinuses were simple creatures and could only manage a word each.

"GREEN!"

"BOTTLE!" They chimed.

"Please can I pick the next song?" said Chloe. Adam's sister trailed behind him, swigging from a water flask. She was as tired as Adam but, as he had not yet suggested they rest, she did not want to either.

"Nope! I've got dibs on 'If You're Happy and You Know It'," laughed Adam. Chloe rolled her eyes. Behind her a large iguanodon crept along, using his large feet and his front claws to pick his way up the precarious path. Dag was strong so despite carrying with him a collection of his cherished tools and inventions, his breathing was normal.

"As long as it isn't 'The Grand Old Duke of York'," he said. "I've heard enough about walking up hills…"

The final dinosaur bringing up the rear was

Oska, an oviraptor. Even though his thin body and his scaly legs were made for running, he was wheezing constantly.

"Can I vote for silence?" he asked. He was the oldest of the group of travellers and was unused to exercise. "I'm finding it rather tricky to walk with all this noise."

"Cheer up, Grandad!" called Tuppence from the front of the group. "I reckon we're nearly there! Maybe another half a day of walking?"

"Anyway, it's only walking forwards. But, you know, up," said Benji. He leapt forward, almost skipping up the path. He was as light as a mountain goat on his feet and just as fearless. Adam's heart skipped a beat when he saw Benji nudge a small rock over the side of the path. It tumbled down the steep mountainside and cracked into two pieces at the bottom.

"Easy for you to say, young Benjamin!" said Oska. "You have younger legs than some of us!"

Benji stopped and turned.

"What, these old things?" he joked. He jumped up and down on the spot in a sort of jig, demonstrating his youth and litheness. The rest of the travelling party laughed, but in his jolliness Benji had taken his eyes off the ground. He slipped on a piece of slate and his leg went from under him.

"Benji!" screamed Tuppence. She reached out to grab him but it was too late; he fell on his front and slid off the path, down the slope beside them and out of reach.

TO BE CONTINUED...

ABOUT THE AUTHOR

From an early age Dan Metcalf knew exactly what he was going to be when he grew up – tall. This was achieved before he even got to secondary school and so another career was decided on. The life of a chocolate teapot salesman is, however, fairly temperamental and so he decided to move to a job which was comparatively reliable – a writer.

He has written for radio, screen and magazines but is best known as the author of *The Lottie Lipton Adventures* (although he is best known around where he lives as 'That Weirdy Beardy Guy'). He is a full-time writer and his biggest ambition is to write a major children's adventure series and create a superhero comic.

We asked Dan some very important questions:

What's your favourite colour?
It's an indescribable reddish-yellow aquamarine green, with hints of eggshell and flecks of grey.

What is the craziest thing you have done?
Give up work to be a full-time writer, obviously.

If you were stuck on a desert island, what item would you want to be stranded with?
A fully crewed yacht.

What's your favourite type of dinosaur?
Iguanodon! They are curious and creative (in my mind they are, anyway) and had thumb-like claws to hold things. That's why I made Dag one in Dino Wars.

If you had a super power what would it be?
How do you know I don't already have one? Alright, then: the ability to soak up a book's information by touching it. Knowledge is power!